KU-369-736

Little Grey Rabbit's PARTY

The Little Grey Rabbit Classic Library

Gift Editions

This edition of
Little Grey Rabbit's Party
has been specially abridged

First published in Great Britain by William Collins Sons & Co Ltd in 1936
This edition published by HarperCollins*Publishers* in 2000

Additional illustration by Mark Burgess

1 3 5 7 9 10 8 6 4 2

ISBN: 0 00 710536 3

A CIP catalogue record for this title is available from the British Library.

The HarperCollins website address is: www.**fire**and**water**.com

Printed in Hong Kong

Little Grey Rabbit's PARTY

ALISON UTTLEY *and* MARGARET TEMPEST

An imprint of HarperCollins*Publishers*

ONE EVENING Hare came racing down the lane and through the gate to the little house at the end of the wood. He was quite out of breath as he dashed into the kitchen, where Squirrel and little Grey Rabbit sat.

"I took a short cut across the lawn of the farmhouse, and I heard a strange noise," said he.

"Oh? What was it, Hare?" asked Squirrel, looking up from her knitting.

"It was a party! I stood up on tiptoes by the juniper bush," ~ Squirrel and little Grey Rabbit nodded excitedly ~ "and I looked through the window. I saw lots of little boys and girls playing games."

"Are they there now?" interrupted Squirrel, throwing her knitting on the floor and springing up.

"Yes. I hurried home to tell you both. I raced like the North wind."

Little Grey Rabbit sat very still, but her eyes opened wide as she heard Hare's tale.

"Let's go and watch them!" cried Squirrel. "We've never seen a party."

They dragged on their wraps and mufflers. Hare jumped up and down crying, "Hurry up! Hurry up!"

He raced along with great leaps down the garden path, and Squirrel and Grey Rabbit hastened after him.

Down the fields they ran, along the narrow lanes, and under the white gate. They ran across the drive to the lawn, and stood under the juniper bush, staring at the darkened house.

Hare walked slowly round the corner and the others trailed after. Then he gave a shrill cry. "Come and look!"

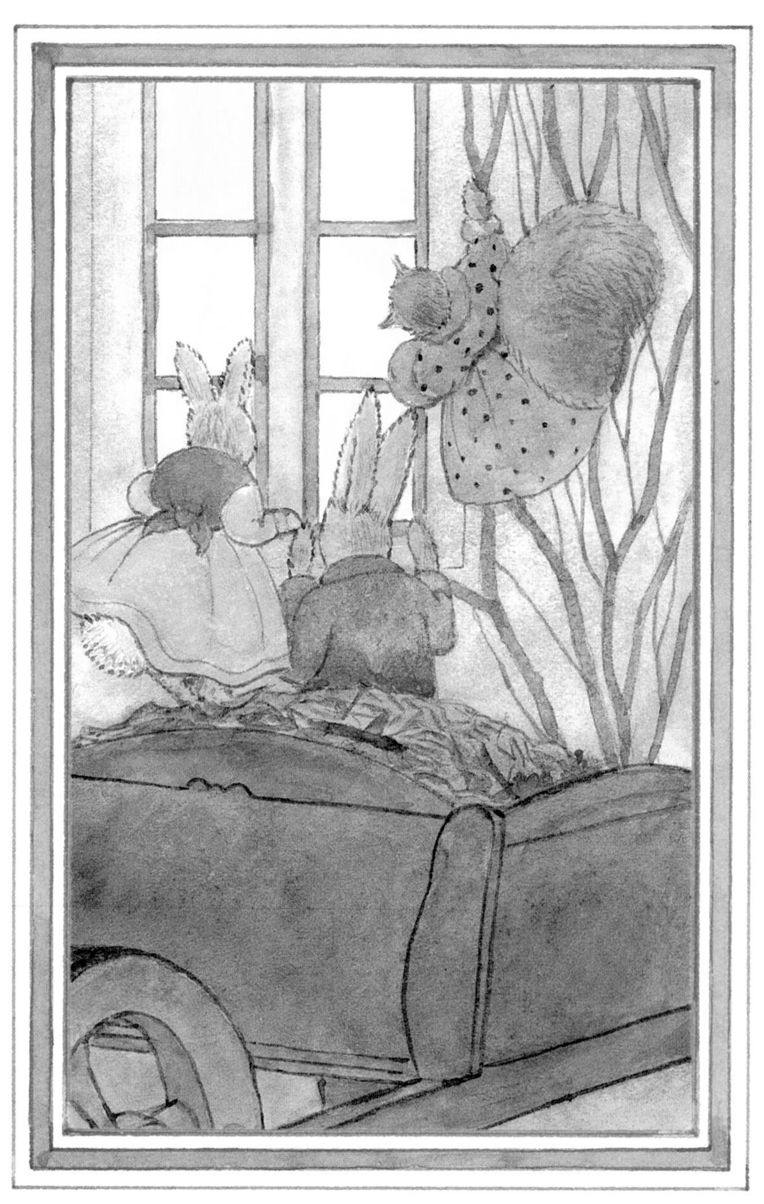

Hare stood on tiptoes, Squirrel climbed a rose bush and little Grey Rabbit scrambled on top of a wheelbarrow.

In the warm, bright room they could see little boys and girls in party clothes playing musical chairs. Then the children trooped to another room for tea.

"What do you think of that?" asked Hare, turning a somersault. "I found it! It was my discovery!"

"It was very clever of you," said Squirrel.

Little Grey Rabbit said nothing, but her eyes shone.

"Why don't you speak, Grey Rabbit?" cried Hare, as she leapt down and trotted silently by his side.

"I was just thinking and wondering and wishing. That's all," she whispered.

Hare dashed off in front, and reached home first.

"Do let's have supper," he said when the others arrived. "That party made me hungry."

So little Grey Rabbit filled their bowls with bread and milk, and they all sat round the table.

"Could we give a party?" asked Hare, sipping from his spoon.

"Why not?" said Squirrel.

"That's just what I was thinking about," said Grey Rabbit, "but I don't know much about such things."

"You had better ask Wise Owl," said Squirrel. "He knows everything."

Grey Rabbit went pale.

"Oh, do! Do! He won't hurt you. You're a favourite of his," they both cried.

So the next day Grey Rabbit went off with a pot of crab apple jelly in her basket.

LAV
ROSE
POPPY
MARS
CAM
CRAB
CRAB
BAY
ROSE
THYME
BAY
OUR

She ran through the wood in the dusk, and rang the silver bell beside Wise Owl's door just as the moon appeared.

Wise Owl put his head out. "Who's there?" said he fiercely, and then, when he recognised the small rabbit, he asked more gently, "What do you want, Grey Rabbit?"

"If you please, Wise Owl," she said, "we want to give a party and we don't know how."

She held up the pot of crab apple jelly, and Owl, with a "Humph" of approval, ate it all up.

"Yes, not bad," said he, and went back into the tree.

Little Grey Rabbit sat waiting and wondering, when the door opened and Owl tossed down a little red book. *How to Give a Party*, it was called.

"Remember to send an invitation," he grunted.

Grey Rabbit pattered off home through the dark wood, with the book safe against her beating heart.

Hare and Squirrel seized the book as soon as she arrived home, and buried their noses in it.

"Come and explain all this to us, Grey Rabbit. The words are so long."

So little Grey Rabbit sat by the fire, warming her toes and reading the party book, and Squirrel and Hare sat on either side of her, crying, "Oh!" and "Ah!" There were Invitations and Thimbles, RSVP and Iced Cake.

"What's RSVP?" asked Hare.

"Rat Shan't Visit Party," replied Grey Rabbit, and added, "I hope my thimble won't get lost in Hunt the Thimble. There isn't another in all the fields and woods."

The preparations began. Grey Rabbit went shopping and

came back with candied peel and cinnamon sticks. Squirrel looked in the little store houses under the trees for nuts. There was such a mixing and tasting, as little Grey Rabbit made her cakes, and Squirrel and Hare dipped in their paws!

Hare ran over the wintry fields and knocked at Mole's back door, banging with his furry knuckles.

Moldy Warp put out his head, stuck his little snout in the air, and asked, "What's the matter, Hare?"

"It's a secret," said Hare, "but I'll tell you. We are giving a party. You are coming, you know."

"Stop a minute," cried Mole. "Tell me slowly."

"No. It's a secret," said Hare. "Goodbye till Party Day."

On the way home he ran into little Fuzzypeg, hurrying back from school.

"We're giving a party, and you are invited," said Hare.

"Oh!" cried Fuzzypeg. "Tell me more."

"No, it's a secret," whispered Hare, and he ran on.

By the time he reached home, he had told his secret to so many, that all over the fields and woods the news spread that Hare was going to have a party.

Little Grey Rabbit took a new goose quill and wrote the invitations on sparkling holly leaves.

Squirrel Hare
and Grey Rabbit
invite you to their party
Full Moon Night
Bring Mugs
R S V P

She gave the bundle of letters to the Robin, and asked him to deliver them.

"Take one to Moldy Warp, and three to the Hedgehog family, and one to Wise Owl, and several to the Brown Rabbits and the Squirrels," said she.

Robin counted the shiny leaves into his bag, and flew off.

The day of the party came. Squirrel, Hare and little Grey Rabbit rose very early as there was still so much to do.

Grey Rabbit decorated the room with red-berried holly and delicate white mistletoe.

There were pink cakes and white cakes, mince pies and sandwiches and roasted chestnuts. In the middle of the tea table was the party cake, covered with ice from the top of the pond. In the centre of it were tiny snow figures of a rabbit, a hare and a squirrel.

When the full moon peeped out from the trees, the three went upstairs to dress. Hare put on his best red coat. Squirrel wore her yellow dress and tied her tail with a blue bow. Little Grey Rabbit draped a scarf of finely made cobweb round her shoulders. On her feet she wore silver birch slippers.

Then she ran downstairs and took a last look round to see if all was ready.

Suddenly she heard a soft shuffle and thump, and she saw Rat's hungry eyes peering in.

"RSVP," whispered Grey Rabbit, but she slipped outside with a herb pie and left it on a stone. Rat sidled up, snatched it and ran off.

Old Hedgehog arrived with a can of milk. "I've come right early," said he, "but I knew you wanted milk for the party."

Soon after there was a knock at the door, and Mrs Hedgehog and Fuzzypeg hurried in. Mrs Hedgehog wore her best silk dress, and Fuzzypeg had new shoes that squeaked.

Mole, in black velvet, followed. He brought a necklace of blue beads, threaded on a horse hair, for Grey Rabbit.

Then came the party of Brown Rabbits and the family of Squirrels. Water Rat followed, handsome in his frills.

"But where's Wise Owl?" asked Hare.

"Owl? Is he coming?" Everyone looked nervous.

"It's quite safe," little Grey Rabbit said. "A party is a truce."

"We are going to begin with Blind Man's Buff," said Squirrel. "Come along, Hedgehog, and be blindfolded."

She tied the handkerchief over Hedgehog's eyes, twisted him round three times and sprang away. Hedgehog groped about the room, catching his prickles in Squirrel's dress, until at last he caught someone. He got Hare.

Hare leaped about, blindfolded, making the rabbits and squirrels scream with delight. Mole tried to slip through Hare's legs, but was caught. Straightaway he caught Grey Rabbit and she pounced on the youngest rabbit.

There was a little sobbing noise under the table, and Grey Rabbit turned up the cloth. Fuzzypeg sat weeping into his new handkerchief.

"Nobody's found me!" he wailed. "I'm nobody's nuffin!" So Grey Rabbit lifted him out and helped him to be found. They all sat down to tea, tightly squeezed against each other in the little room, and Squirrel, Hare and little Grey Rabbit filled the plates and mugs.

Like snow in summer the iced cakes and buns and sandwiches disappeared before the hungry small animals, who had never seen such a feast.

"Wise Owl has forgotten to come," said Hare happily. He cut the big cake and gave everyone a slice with a piece of the cold snow and ice from the top.

Then the door was pushed open and Wise Owl stalked in.

"Sorry I'm late," said he. But everyone disappeared in a twinkling, under the table, behind the chairs, and even in the grandfather clock. Only little Grey Rabbit remained.

"Where's the party?" Wise Owl asked. "Come out! Don't be afraid."

One by one the animals crawled out, looking rather sheepish. The games continued, with Wise Owl applauding solemnly in the armchair as he ate his tea.

"Now we'll play Hunt the Thimble," said Grey Rabbit, and she brought out her tiny silver thimble.

"You hide it first, Wise Owl," said she, and they all bundled out of the room into the garden, where they stood whispering and staring at the bright stars, and the great moon.

Owl looked here and he looked there, but he couldn't see a good place. He took the thimble in his beak, and swallowed it. Then he called the others in, and of course they couldn't find it anywhere at all.

"We give up," they said.

"I've swallowed it," said Wise Owl, and nobody dared to laugh. Little Grey Rabbit nearly cried.

"But-but I can't do my mending now," she faltered.

"But-but we can't play now," said Squirrel.

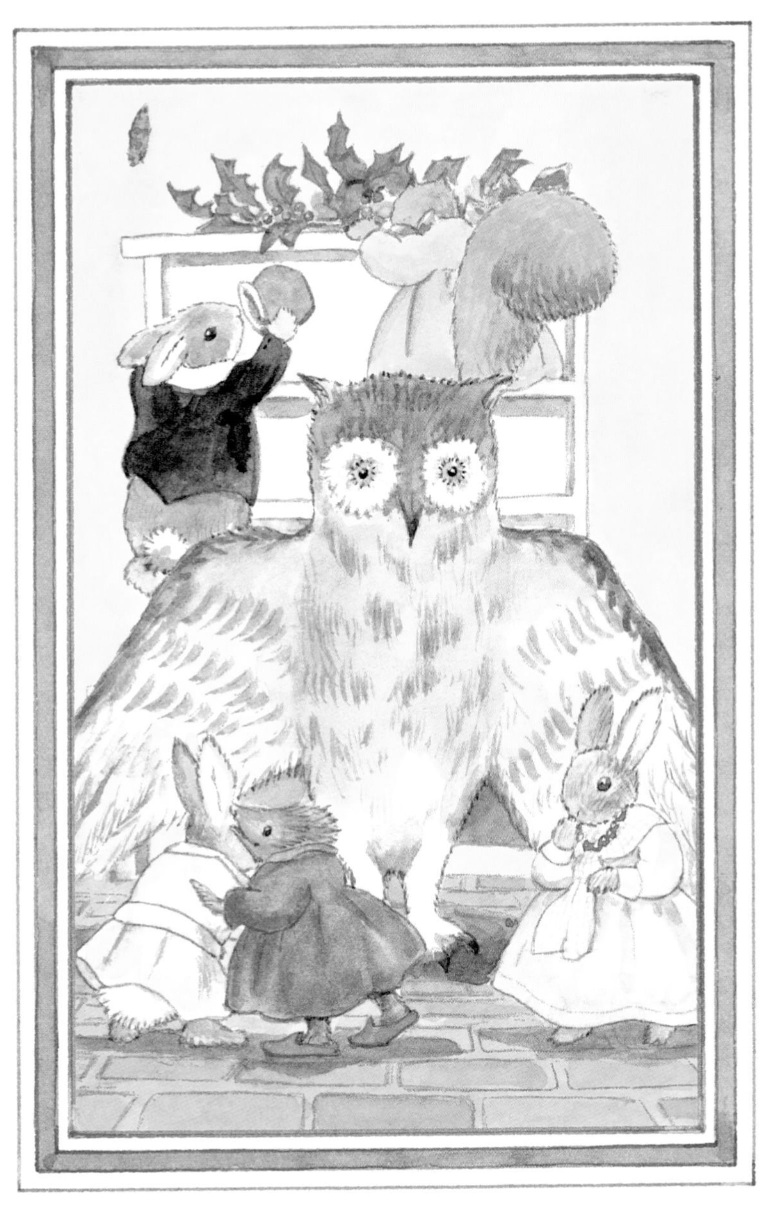

"We'll ask riddles instead," said Wise Owl. "What lives in winter, dies in summer, and grows with its roots upwards?"

They all scratched their heads, but Hare knew.

"An icicle," said he, and Wise Owl stared in astonishment.

"I must go now," said Owl. "I have another engagement."

He waddled to the door. "Thank you for a very pleasant evening," said he, and he flew up into the sky.

Hare mopped his brow and all the animals jumped for joy.

"Let's end up with a dance," said Water Rat. So they danced the polka, and Hare played a jolly tune on his flute.

Then someone looked out at the moon which was sailing high in the sky. There was the Great Bear above, and the gold star, Sirius, beaming down to light them home.

"Goodnight! Goodnight!" they said, as they wrapped their mufflers round their necks and took each other's arms.

"Thank you, Squirrel, Hare and Grey Rabbit for the most beautiful party."

Hare put his flute in its case and Squirrel and Grey Rabbit tidied away the crumbs from the feast. Then upstairs they all went to bed, yawning sleepily.

Little Grey Rabbit opened her attic window and held her beads up in the moonlight so that they shone like blue flames.

"Although I did lose my dear thimble, it was a most beautiful party," she whispered, but only the bare trees and the twinkling stars heard her.